THE LITTLE HUMPBACKED HORSE

THE LITTLE HUMPBACKED HORSE

A Russian tale retold by Margaret Hodges
with pictures by Chris Conover
Farrar · Straus · Giroux New York

Text copyright © 1980 by Margaret Hodges
Based on an original folktale by Peter Pavlovich Yershov,
as translated by Gina Kovarsky
Pictures copyright © 1980 by Chris Conover
All rights reserved
Published simultaneously in Canada by
McGraw-Hill Ryerson Ltd., Toronto
Color separations by Offset Separations Corp.
Printed in the United States of America by Eastern Press
Bound by A. Horowitz and Sons
Designed by Cynthia Krupat
Calligraphy by Jeanyee Wong
First edition, 1980
Library of Congress Cataloging in Publication Data
Hodges, Margaret. The little humpbacked horse.
[1. Fairy tales] I. Conover, Chris.
II. Ershov, Petr Pavlovich, 1815-1869.
Konek-gorbunok. III. Title.
PZ8.H653Li [E] 80-19113
ISBN 0-374-34603-8

For the storyteller
in the kitchen

M H

To my parents,
for the courageous
example they set

C C

OUR TALE BEGINS

Long ago, when the Tsar ruled Russia and peasants worked their small farms, there lived an old man who had three sons. The oldest son, Danilo, was said to be the likeliest of the lot. The second son, Gavrilo, could pass in a crowd without being noticed one way or the other. But the youngest son, Ivan, was thought to be stupid because, when his day's work was done, he seldom rode into town but simply went home, lay down on the stove, and fell asleep at once. He was called Ivan the Fool.

One morning, when the father went into the field, he found that someone or something had trampled down the wheat.

"Watch the field tonight," he said to Danilo. "If a thief is about, we must catch him." But the night was cold, rain began to fall, and, long before midnight, Danilo burrowed into a haystack and slept soundly for the rest of the night.

In the morning, more of the wheatfield was trampled. Danilo poured a bucket of water over his head and pounded on the cottage door.

"Let me in!" he shouted. "I am soaked to the skin! I heard the thief

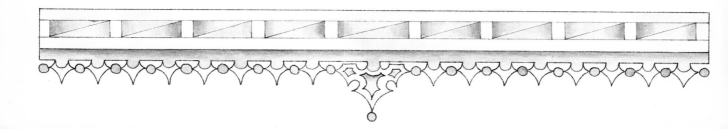

and ran after him for miles, but I could not catch him."

"You, Gavrilo, shall watch tonight," said the father. But this night again rain fell and wind blew, and Gavrilo said to himself, "I may not be as clever as Danilo, but at least I know enough not to catch my death." And he slept the night away under a thick hedge, wrapped in his warm coat.

When morning came, Gavrilo saw that more of the precious wheat was trampled down. So he dropped his coat in the millstream and carried it home dripping.

"What a night I spent!" he groaned. "I caught the thief and wrestled him to the ground. You can see how wet I have been. But the rascal got away all the same."

"It is no use to send Ivan the Fool," the father said sadly. "But come, Ivan. Tonight you will not sleep on the stove. It is your turn to watch the wheatfield, and you must use what wits you have."

That night Ivan took his place in the field and watched the wheat with both his eyes. When midnight came, he saw in the moonlight a mare as white as winter snow galloping across the field. Her golden

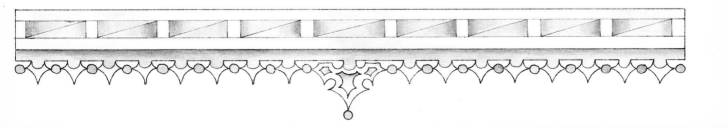

HE FOUND HER WITH THREE COLTS

mane curled almost to the ground. Her tail tossed free.

The mare was feeding in the wheat when Ivan jumped on her back, hind side before. Feeling his weight, the mare leaped away. She raced over the fields, she flew over mountains and forests, she turned and twisted, she reared and kicked. But Ivan held on to her long golden tail and dug in his heels. He would not let go and he would not be thrown.

At last the mare stopped and spoke. "It seems that you are the rider I have been waiting for. Take me home and keep me for three days. Every morning at sunrise, let me roll in the dew, and at the end of the three days I will bear three colts such as you never saw. Two will be fit for the Tsar's stables, if you wish to sell them. But keep the third colt. He will be your faithful friend. All this I will give to you. In return, give me my freedom."

Ivan rode the mare home and hid her in an empty stall where no one ever went, for the peasant had no horse of his own.

"Well, Ivan," said the father next morning, "did you catch the thief? But of course you did not, for here you are, empty-handed."

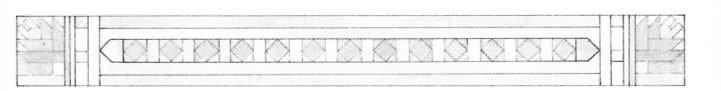

"I did catch the thief," said Ivan. "It was the Devil himself. But I squeezed his neck until he begged for his life. The wheatfield is safe from this day on." He would say no more, and the brothers only winked and laughed at Ivan the Fool.

Well, and so Ivan kept the mare for three days. Every morning at sunrise while his father and brothers slept, he let her out of the barn for a roll in the dew. And on the fourth morning he found her with three colts, just as she had promised. Two had silky coats as black as night. Their manes and tails curled in golden ringlets to the ground. Their hoofs sparkled like diamonds. A real pleasure to see! Both were fine enough for the Tsar's stables.

But the third colt was red and no bigger than a hobbyhorse. He had two humps on his back like a little saddle. His ears were a foot long and stood straight up, twitching this way and that.

"Goodbye, Ivan," said the mare. "These are my gifts to you. Now give me my freedom." Ivan opened the barn door and away she flew, running so lightly that she seemed scarcely to touch the ground.

It was not long before Danilo and Gavrilo saw the three colts.

They paid no heed to the little humpbacked one but said, "Why, here we have a fortune! When the black horses are grown, they will be fit for the Tsar's stables."

"They are mine," said Ivan. Every day he fed the three colts with the best oats. He brushed their coats until they shone, and he led them out to pasture. He taught them to bear the weight of a rider. At last the black horses were fit to carry the Tsar. But the little humpbacked horse remained as small as ever.

One day, while Ivan still slept on the stove, the brothers set off with the black horses to the fair in the capital city. When Ivan went to the barn, he found only the little humpbacked horse, and he began to howl. "Oh, my beautiful horses with golden manes, what devil has stolen you?"

But the little horse spoke to him. "Come along, master. Sit on my back and hold on to my ears. Let us see what we can do together."

Ivan mounted the little horse, thrust his feet forward so that they cleared the ground, and took hold of the long ears. With three whinnies and a kick, the little humpbacked horse flew off like an

A MARVELOUS LIGHT STREAMED ALL AROUND THEM

arrow, and in no time at all Ivan had caught up with Danilo and Gavrilo on the road to the horse fair.

"So, brothers," he said to them cheerfully, "we are going together to sell my black horses."

The brothers were not much pleased to see him and said, "Ivan, you are a fool. Go home."

But Ivan would not, so on they went, all three. As they traveled, the sky grew dark and they had to stop for the night. Suddenly Danilo noticed a fire burning in the distance.

"Go and see what that fire may be, brother Ivan," said he. "You might be able to bring us some kindling." Secretly he thought, "I hope you fall into the fire."

"Yes, go, Ivan," said Gavrilo. "And don't come back," he said under his breath.

Ivan mounted the little humpbacked horse, dug in his heels, and away they flew to the distant field where the fire burned. The nearer they came to the fire, the brighter it burned, until a marvelous light streamed all around them; yet there was no heat or smoke.

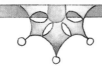

"What wonder is this?" said Ivan.

"A wonder, indeed," the little horse answered. "In this field is a feather of the Firebird. But don't take it. Much, much trouble does it bring."

"We'll see about that," Ivan said to himself. Picking up the feather, he wrapped it in rags, hid it in his hat, and returned to his brothers.

"That fire was nothing but a burning stump," he said. "I could get no kindling." Then he lay down and snored until morning.

Next day they reached the capital city, where word about the fine black horses soon reached the Tsar. He himself came riding into the marketplace, and when he saw the beautiful creatures with their shiny coats and bright eyes and dainty hoofs, nothing would do but he must have them.

While the brothers stood by, Ivan bargained with the Tsar. He sold the black horses for two times five caps of silver coins, all of which he gave to his brothers. They went home and lived happily ever after.

But no sooner were the black horses led away to the Tsar's stables

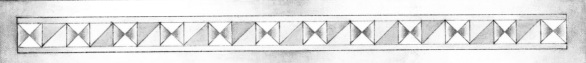

than they tore the reins from the hands of the grooms and ran back to Ivan the Fool. And so they did again and again.

"Since only you have power over these horses," said the Tsar, "I will make you Master of my Stable."

"But mind," said Ivan, "no one must quarrel with me. And they must let me sleep, or I'll not serve."

"Agreed," said the Tsar.

So Ivan the Fool became Master of the Stable. He led the two beautiful horses to the Tsar's palace, and the little humpbacked horse went frisking behind him, clapping his long ears for joy.

The former Master of the Stable was now a mere groom, and he muttered, "Just you wait. I'll get rid of you, little fool Ivan."

He saw that the black horses were always cleaner than clean and their food bins filled with fresh grain, yet Ivan never seemed to do any work. He wore fine robes and bright caps, he ate well, and he spent most of his time asleep.

"The Devil must be doing your work," thought the jealous groom.

TALES ARE TOLD QUICKLY, BUT DEEDS AREN'T DONE SO FAST

One night he hid in the stable, covered himself with oats, and kept watch.

At midnight Ivan came in and took off his cap. From inside his cap he unwrapped—the Firebird's feather. Such a light shone out! Ivan placed the feather in a bin and began to groom the horses. He washed them, he brushed them, and he braided their manes. He filled the tubs with sweet grain. Then, yawning, he wrapped the Firebird's feather in rags again, put his hat under his ear, and lay down to sleep.

As soon as he began to snore, the sly groom slid quietly from his hiding place and crept toward Ivan. He put his hand inside the hat, snatched the feather, and was gone.

The Tsar had barely wakened when the groom entered his bedroom and knocked his forehead loudly on the floor.

"Oh, Tsar," he whined, "Ivan has been hiding a treasure from you. See the Firebird's feather! And what's more, Ivan boasts that he could catch the Firebird itself, if he wanted to."

The Tsar blinked his eyes and marveled at the shining feather. Then he shouted, "Ho! Fetch me the Fool!"

And when Ivan came running, the Tsar shook the feather in his face and screamed, "Peasant, who are you to hide this treasure from me? I should cut off your head! Now bring me the Firebird or you will pay with your life!"

When Ivan heard the Tsar's orders, he began to cry. He went to the stable and told his troubles to the little humpbacked horse.

"Remember what I told you about the Firebird's feather?" said the little horse. "Much, much trouble does it bring. Only get a basket of wheat and soak it in fine wine from overseas. Bring a sack, too. Then let us see what we can do together. But first we must sleep. Morning brings more wisdom than the evening."

In the morning the little horse frisked up his heels and clapped his ears together. Then Ivan poured some fine wine into a basket of wheat and tied it around the neck of the little humpbacked horse. He thrust his feet forward and laid hold of the long ears. With three whinnies and a frisk of his heels the little horse was off and away, over hill and dale, flying over plains, leaping over forests, until they came to a land in the far south.

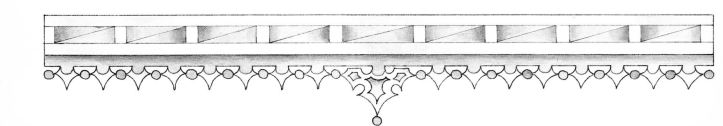

And there, like a wave on the ocean, rose a mountain of the purest silver. On this mountain the sun burned as bright as a candle.

When night came, the little humpbacked horse said, "Now, master, hide yourself behind the basket, but make sure you don't fall asleep. While it is still dark, the Firebirds will fly. They will come to peck at the wheat and they will call to each other. Seize the closest one and hold on tight. Then shout with all your might and I'll appear at once."

Ivan hid behind the basket and lay there like a dead man.

In the middle of the night, light poured out over the mountain as if midday had come, and the Firebirds flew in. They began to run and squawk and peck at the wine-soaked wheat.

Well hidden, Ivan talked to himself. "There must be five plus ten of them! If I could catch them all, wouldn't I be rich! Those red feet! And those tails! Better than chickens, I'd say. And all that light! It's better than the stove back home."

Then he crawled out and seized one of the birds by the tail. "Ho, little humpbacked horse!" he cried. "Hurry up, little friend. I've caught a bird!"

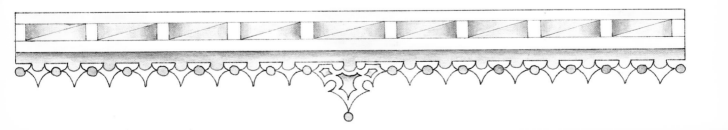

HE SEIZED ONE OF THE BIRDS BY THE TAIL

In one leap the little horse was by his side. Ivan threw the Firebird into his sack and mounted. He thrust his feet forward, took hold of the long ears, and they were off like the wind, over mountains and plains, over hill and dale, until they came to the Tsar's palace. Ivan marched into the royal bedroom.

"Well, did you bring back the Firebird?" asked the Tsar.

"Of course I did," said Ivan. "But before I show it to you, pull all the shutters closed."

Then he put his sack on the table and cried, "Come on out!"

At this, such a light shone forth that everyone covered his eyes, and the Tsar jumped out of bed shouting, "Help! Fire! Call the firemen!" But Ivan laughed until the tears streamed from his eyes, and said, "This is no fire, it's a Firebird. I have brought you a new toy, Your Majesty." Then he went back to the stable with the little humpbacked horse and went to sleep.

The next day the jealous groom again came to the Tsar, calling Ivan either a boaster or a liar, and so it went from day to day. The Tsar, urged by the groom, set ever more difficult tasks for Ivan. But

the little horse always said, "Never fear. We will perform this task tomorrow. The morning holds more wisdom than the evening."

At last the Tsar said, "This Ivan is neither a boaster nor a liar." And he gave Ivan the highest honors and the richest gifts that he could give.

The jealous groom was furious. He thought for a long time. Then he came to the Tsar's bedroom, saying, "When we were all telling stories in the kitchen today, your new Master of the Stable boasted that he could capture the young Tsarevna, whom you have so long wished to marry."

The Tsar was very angry. "What! Ivan the Fool says that he can win the bride whom I have not been able to win for myself? Tell him to bring her here within a week's time or I will cut off his head."

When Ivan heard this command, he went to the stable and wept. "What shall I do? This is surely an impossible task, even for you, my little friend."

"The Firebird's feather brings much, much trouble," said the little humpbacked horse. "But never fear. Only ask the Tsar for a silken tent embroidered with gold, and ask for golden cups and silver plates, and wine and sweetmeats. Then sleep, for tomorrow is wiser than today."

The Tsar granted all that Ivan asked, and the next morning he set off on the back of the little humpbacked horse. They traveled like the wind over fifty lands and fifty seas, until they came to the end of the world, where the sun rises out of the last sea of all.

On the shore of that sea the little horse stopped and said, "Now set up your tent and pour the wine and fill the plates with sweetmeats. Then hide and wait until the young Tsarevna comes. After she eats and drinks, she will begin to sing. Then put your arms around her, hold her fast, and call for me to come. But watch her closely. Don't fall asleep."

Ivan did as the little horse told him to do, and presently the young Tsarevna came over the blue waves in a golden boat, which she rowed with silver oars. When she saw the embroidered silken tent, she beached her boat and sat down in the tent to eat and drink.

Well, and so Ivan was peeping through a little hole in the tent,

"SLEEP ON, IVAN! IT'S YOU THE TSAR IS GOING TO KILL"

but the young Tsarevna was so beautiful that he could only gaze at her. When she began to sing, he fell into a deep sleep, and while he slept, she rowed away.

The west slowly darkened. Suddenly the little horse was neighing over Ivan, pushing him with his hoof. "Sleep on, Ivan! It's you the Tsar is going to kill, not me!"

At this, Ivan began to cry and begged the little horse to forgive him.

"Never mind," said the little horse. "The young Tsarevna will come again tomorrow. But next time you must do better, or you will lose her and your head, too."

The next day the young Tsarevna came again in her golden boat and laid down the silver oars and stepped ashore. But this time, when she sat down in the silken tent and began to drink the wine and eat the sweetmeats, Ivan ran to her and held her fast, all the while calling out to the little humpbacked horse. The young Tsarevna cried and struggled to get away, but when she had a good look at Ivan, she liked him so much that she smiled instead. And when the little

horse came and Ivan mounted on his back, she willingly mounted too, and tucked up her feet. Away they flew over fifty seas and fifty lands, until they came on the sixth day back to the capital city of the Tsar.

Ivan was very sad, because he loved the young Tsarevna with all his heart, but he had to bring her to the palace. The Tsar was happy. "Prepare the wedding at once!" he shouted.

"But I must have my say," answered the young Tsarevna. "You are old. Your hair is gray, and some of your teeth are missing. If you want me to love you, I'll tell you how to become young again. Set three baths in your courtyard. Fill one with ice-cold water, one with boiling water, and one with boiling mare's milk. Whoever steps into these three baths will come out young and handsome."

Well, the Tsar did not much like the idea, but he ordered the three baths to be set and filled. Then the jealous groom came to him and whispered, "Order Ivan to step into the baths first." This seemed like good advice to the Tsar.

When Ivan received the Tsar's command, he went to the stable

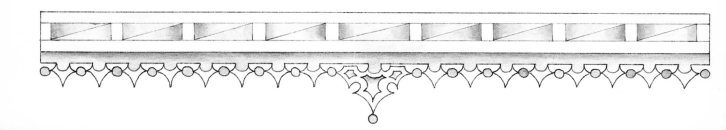

and wept. "Oh, misery! I am about to be boiled!" he told his little horse.

"You should not have taken the Firebird's feather," said the little horse. "Now we have a hard task before us. But never fear. I will take a mouthful from each of the baths and sprinkle you. Then you must leap in at once. All will be well."

Ivan led the little humpbacked horse to the baths. He pulled off his clothes while the little horse put his nose into the tub of ice-cold water, then into the tub of boiling water, and last into the tub of boiling mare's milk. From his mouth he sprinkled Ivan, who leaped into the tubs, one after the other. As he came out of each one, he was more handsome than words can tell.

The Tsar heard the people exclaiming at Ivan's beauty and he came hurrying from his palace. Without taking off his clothes, he climbed into the tub of ice-cold water. But he came out of it older and uglier than when he had stepped in. He put his toe into the tub of boiling water, and fell down dead.

Then the young Tsarevna called to all the people, "Your Tsar had

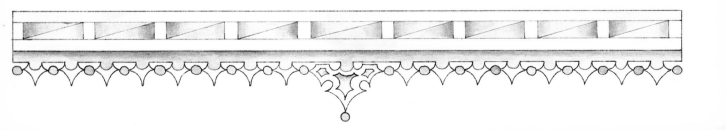

me brought here to rule over you. But I will rule only at the side of
the man who brought me. Will you have Ivan as your Tsar?"

And all the people shouted, "We will have Ivan as our Tsar!"

So Ivan the Fool became Ivan the Tsar, and ruled long and well
at the side of his beautiful Tsarevna. Whenever he had a trouble or
a task, he always talked to his friend, the little humpbacked horse.
And the little horse frisked up his heels and clapped his ears for joy.

N THE TSAR'S KITCHEN THEY TOLD THE STORY OF THE LITTLE HUMP-BACKED HORSE. ONE IS BOUND TO BECOME WISER WITH SUCH A STORY. NOW GO TO SLEEP AND LET ME REST.